Dear Parent:
Your child's love of reading starts here!

Every child learns to read in a different way and at his or her own speed. Some go back and forth between reading levels and read favorite books again and again. Others read through each level in order. You can help your young reader improve and become more confident by encouraging his or her own interests and abilities. From books your child reads with you to the first books he or she reads alone, there are I Can Read Books for every stage of reading:

SHARED READING
Basic language, word repetition, and whimsical illustrations, ideal for sharing with your emergent reader

BEGINNING READING
Short sentences, familiar words, and simple concepts for children eager to read on their own

READING WITH HELP
Engaging stories, longer sentences, and language play for developing readers

READING ALONE
Complex plots, challenging vocabulary, and high-interest topics for the independent reader

ADVANCED READING
Short paragraphs, chapters, and exciting themes for the perfect bridge to chapter books

I Can Read Books have introduced children to the joy of reading since 1957. Featuring award-winning authors and illustrators and a fabulous cast of beloved characters, I Can Read Books set the standard for beginning readers.

A lifetime of discovery begins with the magical words **"I Can Read!"**

Visit www.icanread.com for information
on enriching your child's reading experience.

For Peter

Morris Goes to School Copyright © 1970 by Bernard Wiseman All rights reserved. No part of this book may be used or reproduced in any manner whatsoever without written permission except in the case of brief quotations embodied in critical articles and reviews. Manufactured in China. For information address HarperCollins Children's Books, a division of HarperCollins Publishers, 195 Broadway, New York, NY 10007. www.harpercollinschildrens.com

Library of Congress Catalog Card Number: 75-77944
ISBN-10: 0-06-026548-5 (lib. bdg.) — ISBN-13: 978-0-06-026548-9 (lib. bdg.)
ISBN-10: 0-06-444045-1 (pbk.) — ISBN-13: 978-0-06-444045-5 (pbk.)

16 17 18 SCP 40
❖

I Can Read!™

BEGINNING READING 1

B. Wiseman

MORRIS GOES TO SCHOOL

HarperCollins*Publishers*

Morris the Moose wanted candy.

He went to the wrong store.

5

The man
in the store
said,
"We don't
sell candy.

Can't you read?"

6

Then he showed Morris

the candy store.

The man in the candy store said,

"What would you like?"

Morris looked at the candy.

He liked the gumdrops.

He said, "Give me some of those."

The man said,

"They are one for a penny.

How much money do you have?"

Morris looked. He had six pennies.

"I have four pennies," he said.

The man laughed. "You have six!

Can't you count?

Don't you go to school?"

Morris asked, "What is school?"

The man said, "I will show you.

But first, here are six gumdrops.

They are one for a penny,

and you have six pennies."

Then the man took Morris to school.

The children said,

"Oh, look! A real moose!"

The teacher said,

"Hello. My name is Miss Fine."

The man said,

"He never went to school."

13

Morris could not say anything.

His mouth was full of gumdrops.

Morris swallowed the gumdrops.

Then he said,

"My name is Morris the Moose.

I want to learn to count.

I want to learn to read, too.

I like candy!"

Miss Fine said, "Hello, Morris.

Welcome to our class.

Please sit at a desk."

Morris tried, but he didn't fit.

He had to sit
on top
of the desk.

"We will now study
the alphabet,"
said Miss Fine.
"This is an *A*.
This is a *B*. . . ."

Morris hid under the desk.

He yelled, "Where is the bee?

I'm afraid of bees! They sting!"

Miss Fine said, "I meant
the letter *B*. This one here.
It doesn't sting."
Then Miss Fine said,
"And next there is *C*. . . ."

19

"Oh, I like the sea!" Morris said.

"I love to swim!"

"No, no!" said Miss Fine. "I meant the letter *C*. This one here.

20

And next," Miss Fine said,

"there is *D*, and *E*, and *F, G, H, I* . . ."

Morris yelled, "I have an eye!

I have two of them!"

Miss Fine said,

"I meant the letter *I*.

Morris, please don't

interrupt again."

Morris didn't.

Morris couldn't.

Morris wasn't there.

He had to leave

the room.

One door said BOYS.

One door said GIRLS.

Morris couldn't read yet.

He opened the wrong door.

A girl cried, "Stop!

You can't come in here!

This is for girls.

The other one is for boys."

24

Morris told Miss Fine,

"There is no door for a moose!"

Miss Fine put up a sign.

When Morris came back,

Miss Fine said,

"Now we will spell.

Cat is spelled C-A-T.

Dog is spelled D-O-G."

Morris looked sad.

"What is the matter, Morris?"
asked Miss Fine. Morris said,
"You didn't spell moose."

"Can anyone spell moose?"
asked Miss Fine.

A boy said, *"M-O-S-E!"*

A girl said,

"No, no! It is *M-O-O-C-E!*"

"You are both wrong," said Miss Fine.

"It is spelled M-O-O-S-E."

Morris said, "Oh, I am hard to spell!"

Miss Fine said,

"I think it is time for lunch."

The children opened

their lunch boxes.

 Some of them had
cheese sandwiches.

 Some had cream cheese
and jelly sandwiches.

 Some had hamburgers.

 Each of them had
a piece of fruit.

But Morris had nothing!

He ate lunch anyway.

After lunch the children played.

Some played ball

and some jumped rope.

Morris did both at the same time.

Miss Fine said, "Children,

now it is time to rest."

The children rested on their desks.

Morris tried, but he was too big.

Miss Fine let him use her desk.

When rest time was over,

Miss Fine said, "Wake up! Wake up!

It is time to finger-paint."

Morris said, "I will hoof-paint!"

You can tell which painting he did.

Miss Fine said,

"Now we will study arithmetic.

Who would like to count?"

A boy counted,

"1, 2, 3, 4, 5, 6, 7, 8, 10 . . ."

"No, no!" said Miss Fine.

"Who knows what comes after eight?"

Morris said, "I know! Bedtime!"

"Nine is the answer," said Miss Fine.

"Nine comes after eight.

Who knows what comes after nine?"

A girl counted on her fingers.

"1, 2, 3, 4, 5, 6, 7, 8, 9, 10.

Ten!" she said.

"Ten comes after nine."

Miss Fine said, "That's right."

Morris looked sad.

"What is the matter, Morris?"

asked Miss Fine.

Morris held up his hoofs.

"I can only count to four," he said.

Miss Fine said,

"You can count higher than that.

I will show you."

She counted on Morris's hoofs.

"1, 2, 3, 4 . . ."

Then she counted on Morris's antlers.

". . . 5, 6, 7, 8, 9, 10, 11, 12."

Morris said, "I like to count.

I will never wear a hat."

Miss Fine said,
"Now I think
it is time
to sing a song."

"What is
a song?"
Morris asked.

Miss Fine said,
"I will show you."
She sang:
"I've been working
on the railroad . . ."

"What is
a railroad?"
Morris asked.

"A railroad has tracks,"

said Miss Fine.

"They look like this."

"Oh, I know what tracks are,"

Morris said. "Firemen climb them!"

"No, no," said Miss Fine.

"Firemen climb ladders.

Ladders go up, like this."

Morris said,

"Let's sing another song.

I'm learning a lot!"

Miss Fine said, "No.

We just have time for a game.

Let's play make-believe!"

A girl said,

"I am a TREE!"

A boy said,

"I am

a MONKEY!"

50

Another boy said,
"I am a MOOSE!"
Morris and
the children laughed.

Morris went
to the
coat closet.

He said, "I am a COAT CLOSET!"

The children laughed again.

Miss Fine laughed too.

Then the school bell rang.

Morris asked,

"Is that the ice-cream man?"

Miss Fine said,

"No. It is time to go home."

Morris gave the children their coats.

The children and Morris said,

"Good-bye, Miss Fine."

Miss Fine said,

"I will see you all tomorrow."

Morris ran to the forest.

He took money

from his hiding place.

He wanted candy.

This time he went to the right store.

He said, "Hello.

I want some gumdrops, please."

The man said, "Hello.

They are one for a penny.

How much money do you have?"

59

Morris looked.

He had five pennies.

"I have five pennies," he said.

"Give me five gumdrops, please."

The man gave Morris the gumdrops.

He said, "You have learned

arithmetic! What else

have you learned in school?"

Morris said,
"I learned how to
hoof-paint. I learned
how to spell moose.
I learned how to be
a clothes closet.
And I learned
all the numbers
in the alphabet!"
The man said,
"You mean all the
LETTERS, don't you?"

63

Morris wanted to say Yes.

Morris tried to say Yes.

But Morris couldn't.

His mouth was full of gumdrops.